SPACE WARS

With special thanks to Conrad Mason

ORCHARD BOOKS

First published in Great Britain in 2021 by The Watts Publishing Group

1 3 5 7 9 10 8 6 4 2

Text © Beast Quest Limited 2021
Cover and inside illustrations by Juan Calle
© Beast Quest Limited 2021
Illustration: Juan Calle (Liberum Donum). Cover colour: Santiago Calle.
Shading: Juan Calle and Luis Suarez

Beast Quest is a registered trademark of Beast Quest Limited
Series created by Beast Quest Limited, London

A CIP catalogue record for this book is available from the British Library.

ISBN 978 1 40835 789 7

Printed in Great Britain

MIX
Paper from
responsible sources
FSC® C104740

The paper and board used in this book are made from wood from responsible sources.

Orchard Books
An imprint of Hachette Children's Group
Part of The Watts Publishing Group Limited
Carmelite House, 50 Victoria Embankment, London EC4Y 0DZ

An Hachette UK Company
www.hachette.co.uk
www.hachettechildrens.co.uk

CURSE OF THE
ROBO-DRAGON

ADAM BLADE

ORCHARD

Avantia ...

Once upon a time, it was a lush, green planet with sparkling blue oceans. A haven for life in all its forms, and a home to eight billion people. A place of incredible technology and culture.

Until the Void ...

In Avantia City, it struck on a clear day at the height of summer. No one saw it coming. No one understood it. And no one was prepared.

First there was a roar, like distant thunder. Then a swirling vortex ripped apart the sky, streaked with vivid green and purple storms of electricity. It was vast, like the mouth of a monster.

As earthquakes shook the ground, the citizens scrambled into any craft that could fly. They fled their homes, their very atmosphere ... and from the darkness of space, they watched the Void swallow their planet, leaving nothing behind.

For most, it was the end.

But for those lucky few, the survivors ...

It was only the beginning.

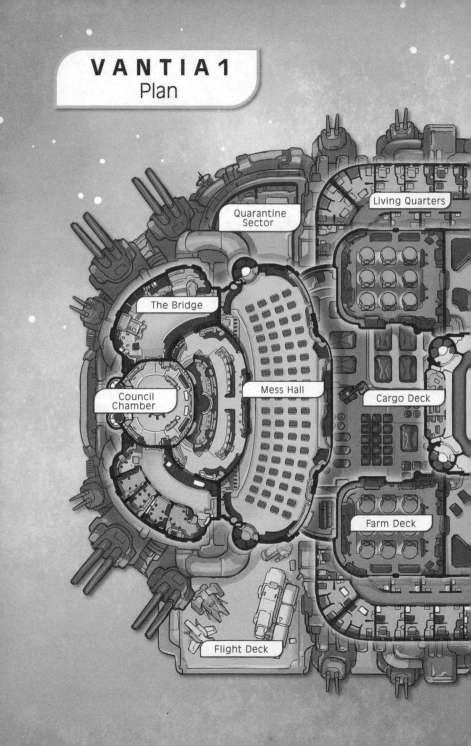

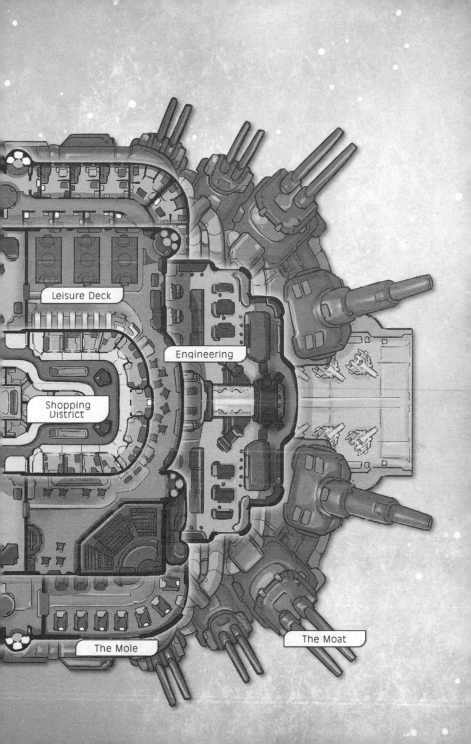

1: Harry Hugo is a talented apprentice engineer, and there's nothing he can't fix.

2: Ava Achebe is a cadet, training to be one of Vantia1's elite space pilots.

3: Zo Harkman, Chief Engineer, has taken care of Harry ever since his parents disappeared.

4: Markus Knox, another cadet, *thinks* he's brave and daring ...

5: Governor Knox is in charge of running Vantia1 and protecting all the station's inhabitants.

6: Admiral Achebe is the commander of the space fleet, and gives orders to the pilots.

CONTENTS

CHAPTER 1

INCOMING!

On the lowest deck of the Vantia1
Space Station, among the crates of
cargo, a small group of labourers had
gathered to watch a slingshot contest.
Harry Hugo loaded a blue energy ball
into his sling's pouch and took aim.
The target was twenty metres away – a

circular piece of scrap metal from the engine of an old space wreck.

"Get a move on!" said one of the other cargo workers, a wiry woman with her hair tied back in a bandana. "Our break will be over soon."

Harry drew the cord back, sighting along it. He was supposed to be running errands for his guardian (and Chief Engineer of Vantia1), Zo Harkman, but when he'd seen the game in progress he'd asked to join. Now he was one more bullseye from winning a stack of credits. Enough to upgrade the jets on his Space Stallion. He could feel several pairs of eyes on him, willing him to miss.

For a moment, the only sound was the

faint buzzing
of the energy
ball, close to
Harry's ear.

He let fly.

Whooooosh!

A streak of blue
light tailed the ball
like a comet as it shot straight and true.

A chime rang out as it hit the target,
shooting off sparks.

"Yesss!" Harry punched the air.

"The youngster wins," muttered a
huge, sweaty man with a scar running
down vertically over one eye from
forehead to cheek. His nametag read
"Jackson". He scooped up the credits in

his tattooed arms and started towards Harry.

"Whoa, there!" The wiry woman stood between the two of them. She nodded at Harry's arm. "Anyone would win with tech like that."

Murmurs of agreement rose from the crowd.

Harry felt his cheeks burning as he glanced down at his sling hand. He'd been born with one arm, and used a state-of-the-art prosthesis he'd customised himself. The hand looked natural enough, with its super-smooth robotics and top-of-the-line synth-skin coating. You could hardly hear the faint whine when he moved his fingers.

But under the black sleeve of his cargo loader's overalls, the rest of his arm was a different story – shining rods of metal, blinking LEDs and interlocking cogs. Harry liked the robotics exposed. It made it easier to tinker, when he had the time.

He would never cheat, though. He'd deactivated any tech that might help right before the competition.

Harry switched the slingshot to his other hand. "How about a re-do?"

The woman's eyes narrowed suspiciously, but she nodded.

Plucking a fresh energy ball, Harry loaded and took aim again.

The silence of the Cargo Deck seemed even more intense this time, as though everyone was holding their breath at once.

Harry realised that he was holding his, too.

"*Harry!*" said a tinny voice. "*Where ARE you?*"

Harry groaned and lowered the sling. The voice was coming over his wrist communicator, and it belonged to Zo Harkman.

"Er ... just got lost," he said into the device.

"*Well, you're wanted urgently on the Flight Deck,*" said Harkman. "*Important job, apparently.*"

"On my way," said Harry. He turned to the workers as he backed away. "Thanks for the game!"

"What about your credits?" asked
Jackson.

"I'll win them back another time!"

He sprinted across the cargo hold,
dodging a huge robotic lifter, then
headed for the Mole dock. Most people
took the 'Mole' to get across the station.
The network of transportation chutes
carried pods between the different
areas, a bit like an elevator, but travelling
in every direction.

An important job on the Flight Deck!
Harry wondered what it could be.
Perhaps he'd be working on a fighter
jet's weaponry, or tinkering with a space
cruiser engine, or even calibrating a
navigation system.

The Mole pod was almost full, but he squeezed in. "Flight Deck, please," he said, and the doors closed before the capsule sped off. The Flight Deck was many storeys up. Harry looked at his reflection in the mirrored wall, and saw he had a grease stain on his cheek. He wiped it with his sleeve, then smoothed down his mop of dark hair.

With a bump, they came to a stop one floor up and the doors opened. Three officials in green uniforms were waiting. They looked at Harry, and one gestured for him to make way. "Wait for the next one, kid."

He obeyed, stepping out. Instead of hanging about, he decided to find another route to his destination. Harry had lived on Vantia1 for eight of his twelve years, since the day the Void swallowed his home planet, Avantia, and took his parents too. Their friend Zo Harkman, now Chief Engineer on Vantia1, had adopted him, so Harry knew more than his fair share about how the station operated. That included all the short cuts and back channels most inhabitants never used.

He'd exited the Mole pod on the Farm Deck, a series of giant interconnected tents where Vantia1's food was grown. Harry hurried along one of the suspended walkways threaded between the multiple platforms filled with greenery – fruits, grain and vegetables to feed the space station's thousands of residents. The air was warm, and filled with moisture as he made his way past the hovering garden-bots that constantly monitored the crops in the synthetic soil and sprayed them with water.

The Farm Deck was hooked up to the same water system that fed the rest of the station, so Harry used a narrow service tunnel through the water treatment facility down to the Leisure Deck, where the 3D cinemas, sports facilities and other recreational activities were based. People were milling about, with four sweaty tennis players leaving one of the zero-gravity courts. A group of kids were queuing to play a space simulator.

Harry boarded another Mole pod, along with several smartly dressed pilots. He was bouncing on his heels, and rushed out in front of them when the doors opened on the Flight Deck, only to stop and suck in a deep breath. Ships of every size and description – from fighters to space yachts, transporters to landing craft, were dotted across the vast hangar. Some gleamed as though freshly painted, others were dented and rusty. It was an engineer's dream, and Harry's eyes drank it in.

"Can I help you?" said a squat droid on caterpillar treads.

"Harry Hugo, reporting for duty!" he said.

The droid beeped, then extended a spindly hand. "You're wanted in the cadet section," it said.

Harry grinned, and headed over. The cadets were the trainee pilots who would one day make up the elite flying force of Vantia1 – those entrusted with the most dangerous and sensitive missions. Only the very smartest and most able kids ever got in. Harry had wanted to sit the tests on his twelfth birthday, but Harkman had refused, insisting he wasn't ready.

"Anyway," he'd said, "what's wrong with being an apprentice engineer?"

"I want to explore!" Harry had retorted.

"There's plenty still to explore in your textbooks!" came the stern reply.

Harry had argued, but his guardian's stubbornness was legendary. If Zo Harkman said "no", that was it. And besides, Harry knew the real reason for Harkman's refusal. He was scared. Scared he'd lose Harry too, the same way he'd lost Harry's parents on Avantia when the Void overwhelmed the entire planet.

As he approached the cadet section, he saw a boy not much older than himself leaning against the side of the cadet carrier, the SS *Nersepha*. The boy was tall, with a sweep of blond hair, and he wore the purple-and-gold uniform of the Cadet Force. *Markus Knox*. Anyone on Vantia1 knew his name, not just as the face of the cadet force, but as the son of the space station's Governor.

Markus rolled his ice-blue eyes at the sight of Harry.

"About time," he muttered.

"Sorry," said Harry. "I was down in Cargo."

The boy's lips turned downwards, as if Harry had said he'd crawled out of a sewer. "Well, you're here now. I need you to look at my seat."

"Your seat?"

"That's right. It's squeaking."

Harry could hardly believe what he was hearing. "Squeaking?"

"Is there an echo in here?" said Markus. "Just sort it out."

Harry gritted his teeth. He knew the *Nersepha*'s systems like the back of his hand. He'd spent hours poring over its plans, dreaming about one day going on board. But not like this. He managed a tight smile. "It sounds like a drop of oil would do the trick."

"Well, does that arm of yours have an oil-dispenser?"

Harry was about to use that arm of his to punch Markus in the jaw when the overhead floodlights died with a *CLUNK*. Everything was black for a moment, before emergency lamps flashed on, bathing the whole deck in red light.

"What's happening?" asked Markus, eyes wide.

Alarms began to sound, and a hologram flickered into life above them. A young female face the size of a small transport vessel, with perfectly smooth skin and spiked white hair, peered down. It was Vantia1's Advanced Diagnostic Ubiquitous Roving Operator (A.D.U.R.O., for short) – an artificial intelligence system which monitored all of the space station's functions.

"Attention all station crew ..." Her voice was as calm as her features. "We have a level 2 debris shower. Please adopt emergency procedures."

The Flight Deck exploded with activity.

Everyone was moving fast, calling out to each other, checking their emergency belts. The belts would activate space suits in case of any sudden hull breaches.

"Don't know why everyone's panicking," said Markus. "The Moat will take care of it."

The communicator at Harry's wrist chimed again. *"Harry? Come in, please. Harry?"*

"Here, Zo," he said. "What's up?"

"Are you somewhere safe?"

"All good," he said, walking with Markus towards one of the large viewing windows that looked out into deep space. "Just about to enjoy the show."

He could already see the incoming

rocks, and they weren't more than a few tonnes each. Debris showers coming from inside the Void were not uncommon, and Vantia1's defence system was always ready. Nicknamed the Moat, its automatic cannons could locate and destroy any threats. Peering upwards, Harry could see massive guns swinging into position already. With a few green flashes, energy bolts zipped through space and vaporised  the rock fragments to almost nothing.

"Bullseye!" whooped Markus.

Harry found himself grinning. Zo Harkman had designed the Moat himself, and it had never let the station down. Then something caught Harry's eye. A single fragment of rock no bigger than his own hand. It struck a bank of satellite dishes at an angle, crushing one like a tin can. It was a one-in-a-million chance.

"That's not good," Harry muttered.

Markus scoffed. "What do you know?"

"That's part of the targeting system," said Harry. "It locates the incoming threats and directs our response."

"How do you know that?" said Markus, looking troubled.

"How do you *not*?" replied Harry.

Markus bristled. "It's over now,

anyway. Time to fix my seat, remember?"

Others were returning to their posts already, and Harry was halfway to the *Nersepha* when A.D.U.R.O. reappeared. "Attention all station crew, we have a level 3 debris shower. Please adopt emergency procedures."

"There's more!" someone shouted.

Harry stopped and turned back to the viewing window. Sure enough, a fresh barrage of rocks was heading their way. And now, just as he'd predicted, the cannons were swivelling aimlessly.

Markus's open mouth and bloodless cheeks said it all.

Vantia1 was a sitting duck.

CHAPTER **2**

EVACUATION

"Targeting systems malfunction," said A.D.U.R.O., as if she was remarking on the weather. "Decks 4 and 5, please evacuate immediately. Five minutes to impact."

The AI's face morphed into a huge timer hovering overhead, giant red digits ticking down, and accompanied by her voice. *4:59 … 4:58 … 4:57 …*

Harry swallowed. Deck 5 was mostly housing and could be repaired, but 4 was the Farm Deck. If that was damaged, the station's food supply would be compromised.

Another voice spoke over the countdown. It was Admiral Achebe, leader of the fleet. Her voice crackled through every communicator on deck. "Combat pilots to the Flight Deck and stand by."

Without the Moat, Harry guessed that the Admiral was planning to shoot down the space rocks with short-range fighter craft. He saw pilots racing across the deck and clambering into their vessels. Part of him wished he could get out there too.

At the same time, looking at the incoming shower, his stomach clenched. *There's no way they'll be able to destroy all those rocks.*

Harry felt a hand on his shoulder, and turned to see Markus. "Where are the escape pods, Robo-arm?" he hissed. "Quickly!"

Harry blinked. "We're nowhere near the impact zone. A.D.U.R.O. said Decks 4 and 5."

"I know that, halfwit!" Markus's cheeks coloured. "I was just … taking precautions."

"Right." Harry shrugged off Markus's hand and headed for the Mole. His mind was racing. Maybe there was still a chance for the Moat to save them. *If I can get to the targeting array ... if I can fix it before the space rocks hit, get the cannons online again ... then, maybe ...*

The countdown continued overhead. *4:09 ... 4:08 ...*

Harry hit the button for Deck 5. Though it was mainly living quarters, it would give the easiest access to the targeting array systems. The silver doors slid shut, and Harry felt the elevator pod rising.

It was silent and peaceful, as though nothing was wrong at all.

But the instant the doors opened on Deck 5, he was back in the midst of the panic. People ran through the corridors clutching cases of possessions. Somewhere a baby was wailing. Through a viewing window, Harry caught sight of the space rocks, and his heart thundered in his chest. They were so much closer now. They were massive, too – some of them must have been thirty metres across. He shuddered at the thought of the devastation they would cause on impact.

He ran faster.

Around a corner, he passed a pair of blue-uniformed engineers. "We could engage the main thrusters," one was saying, "and take the station out of the trajectory."

"It's too late for that," said the other. "They won't fire up in time."

Harry skidded to a halt. Up ahead, he could see Admiral Achebe's red-coated security officers marching down the corridor, clearing out the deck. "Evacuate!" called one. "Evacuate immediately!"

Darting through a side door, Harry waited for them to pass. Then he kept running, his breaths coming hard and fast, until he found himself alone. He tried to imagine a plan of the station. He'd been over the station blueprints a hundred times, in Zo's quarters. There would be an access point somewhere around here.

The countdown, in A.D.U.R.O.'s gentle tones, continued, travelling with Harry wherever he went. *3:20 … 3:19 …*

He knelt by a panel just beneath a snack dispensing console. Rolling up his sleeve, he activated a screwdriver attachment on his arm. With a faint *whirr,* the screws attaching the panel came undone. Beyond this panel was a service hatch that would lead to the targeting systems. If he could reset them, engage backup power …

"Come on, come on," he muttered.

"What do you think you're doing?"

Harry nearly leapt out of his skin.

He turned, expecting to see a security officer. But instead it was a girl his own age, glaring down at him, with one hand on her hip and a small case in the other. She had stern brown eyes, a cloud of curling black hair, and she wore the same purple-and-gold cadet uniform as Markus. He thought he recognised her from somewhere, but her name escaped him.

"I'm ... er ..." said Harry. "What are

you doing? This deck's supposed to be evacuated."

The girl's stare softened. "If you must know, I was rescuing Tiger." She turned the case in her hand and Harry saw a small kitten inside through a grate. "And you?"

"*Harry?*" It was Zo's voice, buzzing from Harry's communicator. He sounded even more anxious than before. "*I'm on the Flight Deck. Where are you?*"

"I'm safe," he blurted out. "Erm ... in my quarters." He gave the girl a pleading look. She raised an eyebrow, but said nothing.

"*Stay there!*" said Zo, abruptly ending the transmission.

"You're Harry, aren't you – you live with Chief Engineer Harkman?"

Harry nodded. He was about to ask her name, when the station shook so hard they lost their balance and staggered.

"First impact," said the girl. "We really should leave."

"There's a manual bypass control system between decks," said Harry. He lifted the panel and set it down. Beyond, the service shaft seemed even narrower than he had expected, and full of smoke. "I think I can fix the targeting array there."

"You *think*?" she said. "That sounds kind of … crazy."

Heart thumping, and without replying,

Harry crawled into the tunnel. He could barely fit inside. Up ahead, an electronic unit sparked. Harry's eyes stung, and his lungs burned. But he held his breath and pushed on through the smoke.

1:13 ... 1:12 ...

At the end of the shaft was another panel. *No time to unscrew this one.* Harry flicked a switch on his arm, routing all power into the hydraulics. Then he clenched his fist.

CLANG! He threw a punch, denting the panel and knocking it free.

Harry scrambled out of the shaft, coughing and blinking. Relief flowed through him to be out of the darkness and the smoke.

Yes! He was in a small cubicle, just as he'd expected. And there was the control unit, up ahead. A narrow viewing window above it looked out on to the debris, still rushing towards Vantia1, now closer than ever ...

The control unit was a bank of flashing lights and switches, all marked with code. In theory, all he had to do was deactivate the system, then bypass the faulty targeting antenna, and restart. But if he got things wrong, it might put the whole system out of action permanently. He was about to begin, when a miniature hologram flickered into life above the control panel. "Attention, Harry Hugo,"

A.D.U.R.O. said. "Your engineering qualifications are insufficient for this operation. Please desist."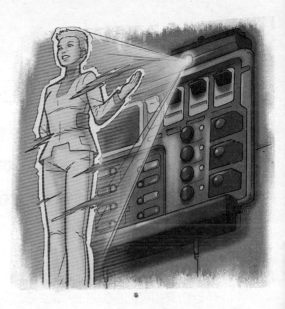

"I'm only going to turn it off and on again," Harry muttered.

The countdown was still speaking distantly. *0:38 ... 0:37 ...*

Harry tripped three switches in sequence on the console. All across it, lights blinked off.

It was dead. He had crashed the system.

0:26 … 0:25 …

Harry pulled the front screen off the console, and inspected the circuitry behind. After a few seconds, he selected two wires and severed them, then linked the ends together.

That should do it …

He replaced the screen and flicked the switch to reboot.

Nothing happened.

Doubt flickered through his mind. *Uh oh. What if A.D.U.R.O. was right?*

Then one by one, the lights blinked on.

0:14 … 0:13 …

"Did it work?" he shouted. *Ten seconds to impact …*

A.D.U.R.O. answered. "Targeting array is

operational. Rebooting Moat systems."

"No rush!" cried Harry.

The station rumbled and groaned, shuddering beneath his feet and forcing him down into a crouch. Harry didn't know if it was the impact of the debris, or the cannons opening fire. He closed his eyes and curled up, half expecting a fireball, or the screech of torn metal, at any moment. When nothing came, he dared to open his eyes. All was silent. He started to crawl back along the shaft, and emerged into the corridor on Deck 5, where the girl stood waiting.

"You did it!" she cried, offering a high five.

Harry returned it. His head was aching, and blood was pounding painfully in his ears – but he didn't care.

The girl's smile drained in an instant, and he realised she was looking at something behind him. He turned slowly to see three security officers, who did *not* look happy. One, with a gold stripe on her cuff, glanced from the loose panel to Harry and Ava.

"I can explain ..." he said. "She had nothing to do with it."

The security officer waved a hand. "Save it, kid." She smiled at the girl. "Miss Achebe, I think your mother will be looking for you."

Of course! thought Harry. *She's Ava Achebe, the Admiral's daughter!*

The officer's glower returned as she pointed at his chest. "You, my boy, are under arrest!"

CHAPTER 3

SPACE PASS

"*You could have* been *killed*!" Admiral Achebe slammed her palms down on her massive granite desk and loomed over it, glaring at Harry and Ava.

Ava's mum had never spoken a word to Harry before now, and he had always been grateful for that. Now her jaw was jutting and her eyes popping with rage.

"Do you have any idea ..." The Admiral tailed off, shut her eyes and ran one hand over her close-cropped hair, as though trying to calm herself.

"I'm sorry, Mum ..." Ava began.

"That's 'Admiral' to you," snapped Achebe. "Governor Knox is not happy about this at all. Disobeying a station-wide directive ... My own daughter! And as for you ..." She turned her fiery gaze on Harry.

"But he saved Vantia1!" Ava

interrupted. "If it wasn't for Harry—"

"Enough!" Admiral Achebe growled, and Harry hardly dared to look at her. "Unless you want to be kicked out of the cadets."

Just then a chime sounded from a hidden speaker. "Enter," said the Admiral.

The door slid open, and Harry's heart sank at seeing Zo Harkman step into the Admiral's office. Even Zo's calm blue eyes had a glint of anger in them, and his normally well-combed grey hair was wild and unkempt.

Admiral Achebe sighed and gestured at Harry. "I'll leave this one to you."

"Come on," said Zo, quietly. "We'll get

a hot meal inside us. Then we'll talk."

★

By the time they reached the mess hall on Deck 2, which was already bustling with the lunch crowd, Harry's stomach was twisting with guilt. Zo had said barely a word the whole way. He settled himself at a quiet table in the corner, then grunted for Harry to get their food.

Harry ordered ramen – Zo's favourite – hoping it would put the engineer in a better mood. Three robot arms whirred away behind the counter, filling the bowls with precise quantities of broth, noodles and vegetables.

"Nice work, kid." The tattooed cargo worker called Jackson appeared at

Harry's side, thumped him on the back and grinned, revealing a gold tooth. "Heard you saved our bacon."

"It was nothing," Harry muttered, sliding the bowls on to a tray and heading back through the canteen.

Halfway there, a foot shot out in front of him. He skipped aside just in time. *Markus.* The boy was sitting at a table of fellow cadets and sneering up at him. "More trouble following orders, Robo-arm?"

This time, Harry couldn't resist the surge of anger. "Did you find an escape pod?"

Markus went bright red and his fists clenched. Another cadet said, "Leave him, Markus. He fixed the targeting array."

"Least he could do," said Markus. "After all, his parents destroyed a whole planet."

Sniggers rose from the tables all around.

Harry's grip tightened on the tray.

"Harry – come here." It was Harkman's voice, calm and commanding.

Markus's grin got even wider. "You going to do what you're told, for once?"

Harry forced himself to ignore the laughter. He stepped round the table and carried the tray over to Harkman.

He had never quite got used to the cold looks, or the whispered comments.

But maybe I deserve them. Maybe the destruction of their home planet really *was* his parents' fault. After all, they were the ones working on unstable scientific research, in the labs underneath Avantia City. It had been one of their experiments going wrong that had somehow caused the Void to appear ... That was what Vantia1's top analysts believed, anyway.

Harry shook his head angrily. No one could know for sure. And he'd only been four years old when it had happened. All he remembered was the wild panic and the rush to the ships as Zo tugged him along. Then, as they left the planet's atmosphere, the great darkness covering everything, swallowing his home.

And his parents with it.

"Ramen?" said Zo, as Harry set the tray down. "Nice try, Harry." But his expression softened a little.

They ate in silence. Then Zo pushed his bowl away and leaned over the table. "Listen. Do you know how lucky you are to be sitting here right now? What you did was unwise, reckless and extremely dangerous."

"I'm sorry," muttered Harry.

"On the other hand ..." A smile flickered across Zo's face. "It was also brave. And selfless. And smart. No one else thought to reset the targeting array. Sometimes the simplest solutions are the best."

Harry's body was flooded with relief. He grinned too. "I learned from the expert."

"Flatterer." Harkman snorted. "Just don't lie to me next time. Are we clear?"

Harry nodded. "Yes."

"Now … Don't think I haven't forgotten your birthday. I know it's a few days away, but … I think you've earned an early present." He reached into his jacket pocket and pulled out a small, gleaming metal card.

Harry blinked. "Is that … ?"

"A Space Pass," said Harkman. Then his hand closed over it, and his expression turned stern again. "But listen – this is a test, Harry. I need you to be sensible

this time."

Harry's heart was thundering with excitement, but he managed to keep a straight face. "I won't let you down."

"Good. And above all ..."

They spoke the familiar warning at the same time. *"Don't go near the Void."*

⭐

Harry whipped the tarpaulin off his Space Stallion and stepped back to admire it.

The vehicle took up most of his bedroom. The whole floor, in fact, apart from the narrow built-in bed, the comms console and the holo-board attached to the wall, which was filled with technical drawings, calculations and discarded blueprints. Zo, who shared the quarters and had a bedroom next door, never asked him to clear it up.

A small hologram of Harry's family hovered beside his bed. His parents, smiling and holding Harry up, giggling and squirming. He couldn't have been more than two years old when the hologram was made.

He tore his gaze away from them and returned to the Stallion. It was the size of a motorbike, all gleaming chrome and bright red paintwork, with a soft, black rubber saddle and handlebar grips either side of the control panel.

No wheels, though. Instead, adjustable thrusters ran along the underside of the craft.

Harry thumbed the ID pad. The bike came alive with a soft buzz, rising from the floor as LEDs flashed on across its body, and the monitor screen glowed with a soft blue backlight.

"Goin' for a ride, H?" asked the Stallion, hopefully.

"Sure are, partner," Harry replied, with a grin. He'd programmed the Stallion with a cowboy speech style. It reminded him of the ancient films his dad liked to watch back on Avantia.

Harry hopped into the saddle,

fastened his space belt and took hold of
the handlebars. With a twist of the wrist,
he engaged the fuel cells, and the bike
thrummed beneath him.

He felt excitement pulsing in his veins.
The Space Pass sat in his pocket, ready to
be used.

"Giddy up," he said softly.

He swung the handlebars, and the
bike turned smoothly. Then he fired the
engines and roared out of his bedroom
door and straight through the main
living area.

He burst into the corridor, slamming
the handlebars to the side and almost
bouncing off the wall.

"Hooligan!" An old woman swatted

furiously at him.

"Sorry!" called Harry, but his voice was lost in the engine's roar as he swerved round her and raced along the corridor.

Instead of waiting for an empty Mole pod, he took one of the service tunnels that spiralled up like a spring through the various levels. His overalls pressed against him as the Stallion sped faster and faster. His face hurt from grinning. How long had it been since he'd last taken the Stallion out for a spin? Months, at least. And since then, he'd turbo-charged the engines …

Racing on to the Flight Deck, he slammed on the brakes and almost went over the handlebars as the welcome droid appeared in front of him, asking his purpose. He flashed his pass and was directed to bay C-15. In the neighbouring bay, a star yacht was docking, one of the astronomically expensive pleasure cruisers that the wealthiest Vantians liked to show off. Harry drifted along its side, then slipped the Space Pass into the console at C-15. The exit light flashed green around the airlock.

Here goes ...

He thumbed the button on his space belt, and the suit activated, spreading like a second skin over his clothes. A transparent helmet sealed over his head, and oxygen began to flow. Then he twisted the throttle all the way.

"Wahoooo!"

Darkness swallowed him as he shot
out into space.

No walls. No
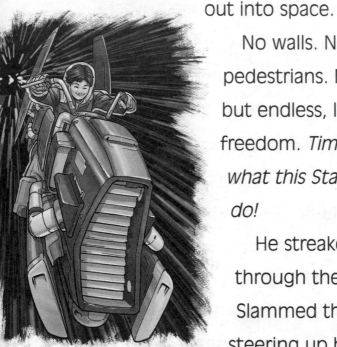
pedestrians. Nothing
but endless, limitless
freedom. *Time to see
what this Stallion can
do!*

He streaked
through the black.
Slammed the
steering up high and
looped the loop, coming
out of it in a corkscrew.

"Clear the area," came an automated

comms message, as he swooped past an observation tower. "You are too close."

He gunned the backup engine, opening it up as he shot away. He felt like the speed of the Stallion might tear him apart.

At last, he pulled up, panting. Hovering in nothingness, he threw a glance over his shoulder.

Vantia1 was surrounded by blackness and a million glimmering stars. Even with nothing to compare it to, Harry could feel its vast size. It was a fortress, its grey outer shell loaded with towers and gunnery, the design inspired by the ancient castles of Avantia's past. It was a safe haven. A city in the sky. You would never have to leave it – and most people never did.

The thought made Harry feel claustrophobic. Turning, he sped out, further into space.

Up ahead, he could see blinking lights. Not stars, but the flashing buoys that marked the edge of the Exclusion Zone.

Zo's words ran through his mind. *This is a test, Harry. Be sensible.*

He slowed as he approached. Beyond the line of buoys was something that made his head spin with vertigo and his stomach turn to water. Something vast, a thousand times bigger than the space station he had just left. It coiled and swirled like a living thing. A vortex that made Harry think of the whirlpools Zo had told him about in bedtime adventure stories, when he was younger.

The Void.

Within it, strange patterns of light flickered and danced. Bright green electrical storms, streaks of plasma and thick clusters of space debris.

Harry's heart jolted as he felt his Stallion shift beneath him. The gravity of the Void was weak here, but unmistakeable. It was hauling him in. Quickly, he adjusted the controls, compensating for the gravity with extra thruster power.

You're not taking me, Harry thought. He glared at the Void, as though it were his enemy. In a way, it *was* his enemy. It had taken his home planet from him, after all.

And Mum. And Dad.

Harry took a deep breath, preparing to swing the bike around and head back to the station, when a strange, blurring shape caught his eye.

It was coming from the heart of the Void, moving so fast it was impossible to tell what it was. Something about it raised the hairs on the back of Harry's neck. It looked organic. *Like some kind of living creature.*

"Engage mid-range scanners," he muttered.

"Sure thing," said the Stallion.

The screen showed nothing, though. They were too far out.

Holding his breath, Harry nudged the controls, pushing closer to the flashing line of buoys.

"We're close to the Exclusion Zone, partner," said the Stallion. "Time to head on back to the ranch?"

Harry wasn't listening. The scanners still read negative.

But as he peered harder at the shifting shape, it seemed to evaporate, turning suddenly into a grey mist. Then that disappeared too.

Weird.

Whatever that was, he could have sworn it was ... *alive.* But that made no sense. That was the whole point of the Void – it killed everything it touched. That's what he'd always believed.

That was how he knew that Avantia was gone.

That his parents were gone.

Nothing could survive there … could it?

"Incoming," said the Stallion.

Harry blinked. Looking around, he saw that the buoys were now flashing red.

Uh oh.

The bike jolted again beneath him, so hard that Harry slipped and had to grip on tight to the chassis. They were moving, being hauled along. But this time they were being pulled out of the Exclusion Zone.

Then Harry saw why, and his blood ran cold.

Just beyond the line of buoys was a patrol vessel. A blue light flickered from its hull-mounted tractor beam, and he was caught right in it. There was nothing he could do as they moved helplessly in towards the vessel.

"Reckon they caught us, partner," said the Stallion.

Harry groaned. "You think?"

CHAPTER 4

QUARANTINE

The disappointment on Zo's face hurt more than the anger in his words.

"I'm sorry," mumbled Harry. "I didn't—"

"I don't need to hear it, OK? After everything I said ..."

Harry nodded miserably. He knew

he'd been an idiot. And thanks to his stupidity, he'd got his Space Stallion in quarantine, where it would be tested for Void-exposure radioactivity.

His heart twisted with guilt. If it hadn't been for Zo pulling strings, Harry would be in quarantine himself right now – or worse.

Zo kept pacing around his engineering lab, brow furrowed. As though he didn't know what to do with Harry.

"I would never have done it," said Harry. "I promise. But I saw something in the Void. Something *alive*."

Zo spluttered. "Impossible!" He shot Harry a glance, and Harry saw that the engineer's expression was not at all certain. In fact, he looked … *afraid*.

"Anyway," Zo went on, "what if it had flung a meteor at you? What if it had simply sucked you in, taken you from us for good? I just—" He broke off, looking suddenly sad. "I just don't want to lose you, Harry. Not you too."

Harry's mouth went dry. He tried to speak, but the words wouldn't come.

Zo's communicator crackled.

"Chief Engineer, please attend Council Meeting 902.093," the placid voice of A.D.U.R.O. said.

Zo sighed heavily. "We'll talk more about this later," he said.

As Zo turned to find his jacket, Harry caught sight of a piece of material

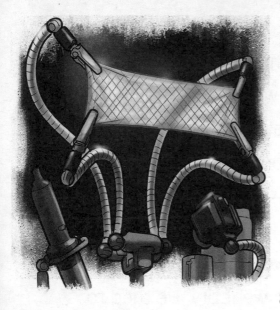

stretched out and clamped in robotic pincers at a workstation. It was silvery but translucent, and it made him think of snakeskin. He had never seen anything like it before.

"Hey, what's this?" Harry asked.

Zo was already walking to the door. "Oh, nothing interesting," he said, switching off the lights. "Next shift isn't for a few hours, right? Why don't you go and hang out on the Leisure Deck?"

✪

Harry spotted Markus the moment the doors opened on the Leisure Deck. The cadet was playing a round of anti-grav disc with some of his cronies, all in uniform.

Harry tried to skirt round, keeping his head down. But Markus had seen him too.

"Hey, look who's back from outer space!" whooped Markus. "Next time, why don't you trot your little space pony right into the Void? Maybe you'll find your parents there!"

Harry stopped, feeling a hot surge of anger. "I saw something!"

"Ooooh!" said Markus, lifting his eyebrows in mock astonishment. "I didn't realise you *saw* something!"

"Space ghost, was it?" sneered one of Markus's friends.

Several of them snorted with laughter.

"Hey!" Harry turned to see Ava approaching, fists curled. "Can it, Markus. It's time for the training exercise on the *Nersepha*."

"Oh what, is Harry your boyfriend now?" said Markus.

"Ava's boyfriend is a dirty grease monkey," jeered another of his crew.

"And all his friends are space ghosts!" added Markus. He waved his arms as though he was spooked, and as he did so, the light caught a flat, rectangular object poking from his breast pocket.

If that's what I think it is ...

Harry knew just what he had to do.

He lunged forwards, feeling a twinge of triumph as Markus's eyes widened. Then he slammed into the cadet, and they both went sprawling across the deck.

Harry grabbed at Markus's uniform, tugging free the object he had seen. His ears were filled with the whoops and cheers of Markus's friends, all watching with delight.

"Fight!"

"Robo-arm's blown a fuse!"

"Get him, Markus!"

Harry fought to hold Markus down, but he wasn't strong enough. Markus

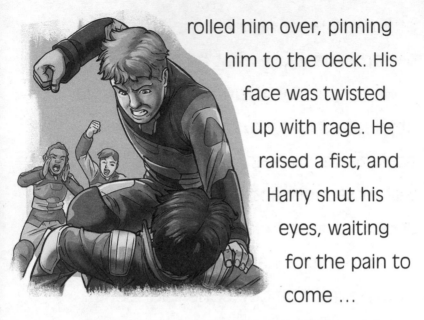

rolled him over, pinning him to the deck. His face was twisted up with rage. He raised a fist, and Harry shut his eyes, waiting for the pain to come …

Then he felt the weight of the older boy lift from his body. When he looked again, he saw that Ava and another cadet had hauled Markus away.

No time to lose.

Harry scrambled to his feet, glancing back once as he darted for the Mole dock. The last thing he saw was Markus's bright red face, spitting insults, before the doors closed with a soft *ding*.

Harry's fingers uncurled from the object he'd taken from the cadet's pocket. *Yes!* Just as he'd thought. It was a silver security pass, several clearance levels higher than his own. Harry selected the Quarantine Sector on Deck 8.

I'm going to prove what I saw was real.

So long as his Stallion's scanners were calibrated, it should have recorded everything – including the strange shape Harry had seen in the heart of the Void. All he had to do was to get to the craft and access its logs.

The pod arrived, and he stepped out into the Quarantine Sector. Bay doors stretched out along the corridor, each one heavily reinforced with small plexiglass viewing windows. He waited, tense and listening. If he was spotted now, no pass or excuses would get him out of trouble.

Satisfied there was no one around, he set off down the corridor, checking the bays as he went. At the fourth one along, he saw what he was looking for. He held the pass against the door scanner.

With a *clunk*, the door unlocked, then slid open.

The bay was a bare and pristine white room, like an operating theatre, and Harry's Space Stallion was the only object inside. The back of his neck prickled, and he cast another quick glance behind him, before slipping inside.

He thumbed the ID panel, and the Stallion rose almost silently into the air, LEDs flashing. "Mighty fine to see you, partner," it said. Harry almost thought it sounded relieved. "This here stable gives me the creeps."

Harry grinned. "Sorry, partner. You've got to stay here a little longer. Just need to access your feed."

He tapped at the control screen, and in moments, the recording was playing, a flickering miniature hologram of the Void spinning just above the handlebars. *Yes ...* There it was. The strange, coiling grey shape that Harry was sure he'd seen. *So I didn't imagine it ...*

He copied the recording to one of the Stallion's removeable chips, slid it out and tucked it in his pocket. Then he turned to go.

And gasped.

Standing in the doorway, hands on hips and surrounded by security officers, was Markus. His face was lit up with triumph.

"What's the matter, Harry? Did you think you'd been clever?" He leaned forward, snarling. "My pass is trackable, genius. And now you're in trouble. *Serious* trouble. What do you think you'll get for theft from an officer? Exile to a mining colony?"

Harry had to admit, things didn't

look good. *Arrested three times in one day* ... There was no way Zo would be so understanding this time.

But he wasn't going to show Markus that he was rattled. "You're not an officer," he said.

Markus's grin faltered, but only for a moment. His communicator told him he was needed on the SS *Nersepha* at once with the other cadets – it was ready to launch.

"Guards!" he said. "Seize him."

CHAPTER 5

INTRUDER ON
DECK 1

Strong arms pushed Harry down
the corridor. "Wait!" he said. "You don't
understand. I saw something in the Void!
Something dangerous!"

But the security officers ignored him.
In the distance, Harry could hear the

sound of Markus laughing.

His heart sank at the thought of Zo finding out that he'd been caught – *again*.

"Please," he tried. "If I could just speak to the Governor … Or Admiral Achebe. Or—"

"Quiet now," growled one of the officers. Harry was shoved into the Mole pod once more, surrounded now by four security personnel. The lead officer asked the pod to take them to the brig. Vantia1's prison was located right in the centre of the station, with no windows.

They shot off.

Harry stole a glance at the man beside him. He looked almost bored. Harry knew the security rotas – these guards must be at the end of a long shift.

Which meant they might be tired. *Maybe not at their sharpest ...*

Harry felt his body tense. Was he going to do this?

One thing was for sure – if he got locked up in the brig, he couldn't explain what he'd been doing on the Quarantine Deck. He couldn't show Zo the recording. And who knew how long it would be before A.D.U.R.O. processed his case file?

Harry swung his foot and kicked the emergency stop on the pod.

Screeeeech! The capsule squealed to a halt. The guards weren't ready and three of them toppled to the ground with cries of shock. One grabbed Harry's prosthetic arm as the doors popped open. He

administered a mild electric shock, which threw the guard off, then stopped to grab his security pass.

"Hey!"

Harry ran out, ignoring the officer's shout.

He found himself in the Shopping District on Deck 3. At the end of a corridor he stumbled out on to a balcony overlooking a mall, brightly lit in neon colours and crowded with Vantians. The enormous hall echoed with conversation, music and the whirring of robotic shop displays.

Now he just had to work out the quickest way to the Council Chamber. It was on Deck 1, at the very top of the space station, and if he got there – if he could speak to the Governor – even Security couldn't touch him.

"Stop!" Boots pounded the metal behind him.

Harry ran.

He slid down the rail of an escalator, ducked low and tried to lose himself in the crowd. Glancing back, he saw the security guards following. They were scanning the mall, so Harry guessed they'd lost sight of him – for now, at least.

Sneaking to the edge of the concourse, he slipped into a clothes shop. The far wall showed a vidscreen playing an advert for Rocket Hoppers, the latest thruster boots, and the sort of thing he would never be able to afford. In front of it was a rack of workers' overalls. Harry slid behind it. Outside, he could hear security officers questioning passers-by, and his heart beat faster.

Had he just run straight into a dead end?

"Hello, Harry Hugo," said A.D.U.R.O.'s voice. Harry nearly jumped out of his skin. A.D.U.R.O.'s face had appeared on the shop's vidscreen, replacing the ad. "Please surrender yourself."

"I'd rather not," said Harry. He pulled off his wrist communicator, which contained a tracker, and tossed it aside.

The image flickered. Then through the window Harry saw A.D.U.R.O.'s face reappear, a thousand times larger, on the giant vidscreen ceiling overlooking the concourse. "Attention, Security Operatives. Harry Hugo was last spotted in Store A-42."

Harry groaned.

Then his gaze fell on a pair of silver boots in the shoe section. Rocket Hoppers. The real thing! They were bulky with wiring and twin engines, and red

Fireflash logos were painted on the sides.

He sprinted over, grabbed the boots and the control glove, and pulled them on. A droid floated over. "Would you like me to find a pair your size, sir?"

Harry activated the boots with the gauntlet.

Whooooosh ... The power of the boots took him by surprise. He roared upwards and slammed his skull against the ceiling. *THUMP!*

Head ringing, he flicked his heels to redirect his flight path. He swept through the store, knocking a rail of coats down and almost smashing into the window.

Then he was out, soaring over the heads of the crowd. Shouts rang out below him.

"There he is!"

"Bring him down!"

Harry winced as a stun ray beam sliced the air beside him, close enough to feel its heat.

He tucked his arms in, trying to make himself as streamlined as possible as he shot towards the far balcony. He was working every muscle in his body to keep himself going straight, and he was still wobbling.

Rocket Hoppers are way harder than

they look in the ads!

He arced over the balcony and killed the thrust. At once, he dropped, landing off balance and rolling head over heels. Still dizzy from the impact with the ceiling, he tugged off the boots.

Up ahead was a Mole dock. *Finally, some luck.* Harry's heart sang as he staggered into the pod. "Council Chamber, please." He swiped the pass over the reader. As the doors slid closed, he caught one last glimpse of the officers, just reaching the top of the escalator to the balcony.

He slumped down, gasping for breath. *That was close ... Too close.*

But before he'd had a minute to

recover, the doors slid open on Deck 1, revealing a short, red-carpeted corridor ending with the smooth metal doors to the Council Chamber. There was not a guard in sight. There didn't need to be. No one could even access this level without the right clearance.

Harry ran along the corridor, and tumbled through the doors.

He had never seen the Chamber before in the flesh. It was a large, round room, its red carpet emblazoned with the golden phoenix emblem of Avantia. A row of portholes on one side gave a view of deep space.

"Harry?"

It was Zo Harkman. He sat in one of

ten red leather swivel chairs positioned around a large holo-table.

"What's the meaning of this?" The new voice belonged to Secretary Bremmer, a short, scowling man dressed all in black. He was Governor Knox's right-hand man.

The other chairs were all occupied by the council members, including Governor Knox herself, and Admiral Achebe. She looked as though it was all she could do not to stride over and wring Harry's neck.

Everyone was staring at him.

Harry's face flushed, and his confidence left him. His stomach turned to water.

Governor Knox watched him, hawk-like, from the largest of the armchairs. Her badge of office glinted gold on her long purple robes.

"Security," the Governor's secretary muttered into his communicator. "Intruder in the Council Chamber."

"No! Wait!" Harry yelped, before he could think it through. "There's something I have to tell you."

Bremmer's scowl grew even darker. "*You?*" he sneered.

"Let him speak, Bremmer."

Everyone turned at Governor Knox's voice. It was quiet but commanding – a voice that was impossible to ignore. *She's really nothing like her son.*

"I've heard rather a lot about this young man today," said the Governor. Harry thought – or hoped – he saw the ghost of a smile

twitching at the corners of her mouth. "Let's see what he has to say for himself."

Harry caught Zo's eye. The Chief Engineer was ashen-faced. But he nodded.

Heart beating faster than ever, Harry crossed to a terminal at one side of the room. His hands shook as he slotted the

Stallion's data chip in.

The room grew dark. Then a huge hologram began to spin just above the council members' heads. It was the recording of the Void, and the strange, shifting object at the heart of it. "I saw this," said Harry. "Out by the boundary, just a few hours ago."

The silence seemed to last for ever. Harry held his breath.

Then, at last, the Governor spoke. "It looks like ... a dragon."

The chamber exploded with voices, all raised in alarm.

"It can't be!"

"... never seen anything like it ..."

"... check the scan logs ..."

Harry wanted to feel relieved. But seeing everyone panicking made him feel even worse. *What is that thing?*

At last the Governor raised a hand, and silence fell again. "Remain calm," she said sternly. "In all likelihood, this is simply a mirage, or even some form of debris. There is no need to alert the other stations just yet."

"The Moat is fully operational again," said Admiral Achebe. "And I'll send extra patrols out around the Exclusion Zone."

"Very good." Governor Knox turned her ice-blue eyes on Harry. "Thank you, young man. But next time, please think twice before interrupting the Council."

Harry frowned. "I don't understand."

"Harry ..." rumbled Zo.

"But why aren't you worried?" Harry couldn't seem to stop himself. "Don't you know what this means? If there's something living in the Void ... then maybe there are Vantians in there, too! There could be *survivors*, there might be—"

"Enough," said the Governor. Her gaze softened. "I'm sure Chief Engineer Harkman here has warned you before about the danger of leaping to conclusions."

Harry didn't know what to say. He opened his mouth, then closed it again, hope leaking out of him.

Just like that, it was all over.

Then the hologram vanished.

A.D.U.R.O.'s huge face appeared instead, hanging above them. It was flashing red, bathing the council chamber in its light.

"Emergency broadcast detected," said A.D.U.R.O. "Source: cadet transport craft SS *Nersepha*."

"Display," snapped Admiral Achebe. Her eyes were wide with fear. *Ava is on board that transport*, Harry remembered. They could only just have launched.

As if in answer to his thought, Ava's own face replaced A.D.U.R.O.'s. She looked frightened. "SOS," she gasped. "We're under attack! Losing power. Void gravity has got us, and we're drifting towards the Exclusion Zone. Transmitting co-ordinates now." A series of letters and numbers flashed through the air.

Ava hesitated, as though afraid to go on. "The attacker, it's … I don't know *what* it is. It's like nothing we've ever—"

The image died. The red light shut off. And there was nothing but empty space beyond the plexiglass dome.

The silence was even longer this time.

Harry's mouth had gone dry. *What did she mean, 'attacker'?*

There was no time to wonder, though. Because there was another, even greater danger. *If we don't do something, the SS* Nersepha *will be sucked straight into the Void …*

CHAPTER **6**

ABANDON SHIP!

"*Scramble response ships,*" ordered Governor Knox. Her voice was calm as ever, but Harry could have sworn her face was a shade paler.

Admiral Achebe turned away, talking rapidly into her communicator.

It's like nothing we've ever seen. That

was what Ava had been about to say. And Harry couldn't help thinking of the strange shape twisting and coiling in the heart of the Void.

Why didn't the scanners pick anything up?

"I've sent my best engineers to the Flight Deck," said Zo, looking up from his own communicator. "If we can get them on board the *Nersepha*, they can fix the problem."

"I'm coming too." The words came out of Harry's mouth before he could think it through. "I know that ship. I've studied the blueprints."

"Harry …" began Zo.

"Let him," said Admiral Achebe.

"Please, Harkman. If what the boy says is true ..."

Zo looked uncomfortable, but in the end, he nodded.

Harry's heart fired with a mixture of excitement and pride.

And fear.

"Enough talk," barked the Admiral. "To the Flight Deck!"

✪

Minutes later, Harry was locking his space belt in the cramped rear section of an Intercept IV. The zippy short-range vessels were mainly for ferrying personnel between larger craft or space-docks, but they were top of the line, and some of the fastest ships on Vantia1. *The*

Admiral is throwing everything she's got at this problem.

Achebẹ herself dropped into the pilot's seat and began tapping at the controls. Screens lit up all around her, warning lights flashing, diagnostics humming.

Harry tried to breathe, regular and calm. But it was impossible to focus. The six best engineers on the station were strapping up all around him. And they were about to set out on a dangerous rescue mission, to the edge of the Exclusion Zone …

"Engaging thrusters," said the Admiral. "Sit tight."

The whole vessel vibrated, rattling

Harry's teeth and filling his ears with the roar of the engines.

Then his stomach lurched as the Intercept IV bolted out of the airlock like a laser-guided missile.

The viewing windows filled with the darkness of space. Harry saw the blinking buoys at the boundary, racing towards them. At the very edge of it, Achebe pulled up, hovering.

Harry spotted the SS *Nersepha*. It was a floating dot at first, but grew larger as they approached. Its thrusters were dead, and Harry couldn't see any other signs of power on board. His heart pounded.

Achebe's brow furrowed in thought.

"Tractor beam?" Harry asked.

One of the engineers shook his head. "That vessel's too massive, even if we use full power."

"We have to get on board," said another engineer. "Evacuate the cadets and bring it back ourselves."

"We can use a docking tunnel to link the two ships," said Admiral Achebe. She nodded, satisfied. "I'm going in."

Harry had to admire the Admiral's piloting skills. As graceful as a ballet dancer, she spun the ship, powering gently until the Intercept IV was nestling up alongside the *Nersepha*'s hull.

"Deploying tunnel," said Achebe.

Harry watched in fascination as the segmented tube extended from the side of the Intercept and locked on to the *Nersepha*'s emergency hatch. With a hiss of hydraulics, the Intercept's own hatch opened, creating a passageway between the vessels.

"Higgs, Adeyemi, Rossi. You're with me," said the Admiral. "The rest of you, get going."

Harry followed the other three engineers. They had to crouch and scuttle along the tunnel. But in no time, they were on board the *Nersepha*.

The ship was in complete darkness.
Not even an alarm sounding. They flicked
on their shoulder flashlights.

"Even backup power is down,"
muttered an engineer whose tag read
"Beck".

"Wait," whispered Harry. "Do you hear
that?"

They froze, not daring to breathe.
There it was again – voices raised. *Calling
for help* ...

Harry ran with the others, pools of
light bobbing ahead of them.

Two of the engineers had to heave
open the doors to the cockpit. But once
they were through, they found the

cadets all clustered together by the main console. They threw up their arms to shield their eyes from the flashlights.

"Who are you?" squealed Markus. "Stand down!"

"They're Vantians," snapped Ava, failing to hide her irritation. She caught Harry's eye. "We've tried to figure out why the power's down, but we're not engineers."

"Leave it to us." Harry darted to the console and got to work, trying to engage backup power, while another tech called Dobbes examined the emergency fuel cells.

"Forget about that!" said Markus. "We need to get back to the station!"

"Give them time," growled Ava, sounding just like her mum. "If we can save the ship ..."

"What happened?" asked Harry.

Ava shuddered. "Some kind of attack. There was a bright light ... Something overloaded the system."

While the other two engineers began ushering cadets from the cockpit, Harry's console flickered on in power-saving mode. Dobbes had managed to hook up the fuel cells.

"Report," ordered Admiral Achebe, over Harry's communicator.

"Doesn't look good," said Harry. "Hull's breached. We'll need to fix it externally before we can re-engage the power."

"Negative," said the Admiral. "It's too risky – abandon ship."

"Copy that," said Ava. "Coming, Harry?"

But before he could reply, the communicators crackled into life again. "Scanners are detecting something." The Admiral's voice was taut with panic. "Incoming. Get out of there!"

Ava grabbed Harry's arm and hauled him away.

They stumbled from the cockpit into an empty corridor. *The other cadets must have already evacuated*, thought Harry. They ran, boots clanging on metal, picking up pace until the ship tilted, groaning and rumbling all around them.

SLAM! They lurched sideways, smacking into the wall and sprawling on the floor.

"What was that?" gasped Harry, head spinning as he picked himself up.

"Some kind of impact." Ava's eyes were bright and wide in the glow of Harry's flashlight. "It's just like what happened last time."

"Ava! Harry!" Admiral Achebe's voice sounded desperate over the communicator.

"Here," said Ava. "What's wrong?"

"The docking tunnel has been breached. It's not safe to use. Stand by, I'm calling in another ship."

Harry and Ava looked at each other.

Harry knew they were both thinking the same thing. *There isn't time for that.*

"We're too close to the Void now," said Ava. "It'll suck us in."

"Then there's only one thing for it." Harry tried to sound more confident than he felt. "We'll have to fix the hull and repower the vessel."

Ava closed her eyes, taking a deep breath. "Mum … Get the others back to Vantia1."

"I – I'm sorry." The Admiral's voice sounded broken. As though she was trying to hold back the tears. Harry could see that Ava was too.

"Come on," he said quickly. "It's a two-person job."

Staying close beside one another in the darkness, they ran through the corridors to the section where Harry had detected the breach. Ava stopped at the airlock. "Skins?"

Harry nodded.

Together, they pressed the buttons on their belt buckles. The spacesuits inflated from their uniforms, covering every bit of exposed flesh in clear material.

Harry unhooked an emergency cord from its housing on the wall, and they looped it through their belt buckles. It would keep them attached to the ship at all times.

Then they opened the airlock and let themselves drift out into space.

Harry tried to ignore the vertigo that swelled in his stomach. It was one thing to fly a ship out here in space. But to be floating free in zero gravity, with only a high-tensile cord to keep him from drifting off into the vast, swirling mass of the Void …

Forcing himself not to look at it, he clung to the handles on the exterior of the hull as they made their way to the site of the breach. A short distance away, he could see the

Intercept IV pulling away, the ruined docking tunnel hanging limp and torn from its hull.

"What is *that*?" Ava's voice came through his communicator. She was looking at the hull. There were three giant rips in the metal shell of the *Nersepha*, each longer than a person. "Those are—"

"Claw marks," finished Harry.

Governor Knox's words came back to him. *It looks like a dragon.*

"How are we supposed to patch that up?" asked Ava.

But Harry wasn't listening. Something had flickered at the corner of his vision. And when he turned to look, all the breath left him at once.

It was coiling towards them, rounding the bow of the SS *Nersepha*. It was immense, bigger than the cadet transport. But it moved fast, winding like a snake through grass. Like something alive.

It can't be ...

His stomach clenched. He gripped Ava's arm, and felt her tense as she saw it too.

"Is that what I think it is?" she breathed.

Its body was muscular and sinuous, covered in overlapping silvered plates, like scales. There were flecks of other colours too – oranges and reds – and a tail streamed out behind it, like a streaking comet. Its vast wings beat silently in the endless darkness of space.

And its face ... Horned and twisted into a savage snarl, with eyes that glowed red like coals, and jaws that snapped like a crocodile's, showing sharp, glinting teeth ...

It was a thing that belonged in museums back on Avantia; or in the bedtime stories Zo had told Harry when he was little, of Beasts and heroes who carried swords. Not here, in real life.

A dragon!

"Let's go," croaked Harry.

But it was too late. A torrent of plasma spewed from the creature's jaws,

bathing the bow of the *Nersepha* in crackling blue light.

Harry jerked back, pulling Ava with him. The heat was intense, even through the space-skins they wore. He could see the metal shell of the craft bubbling, burning white-hot, so bright he could hardly look at it.

Then slowly, as though in a nightmare, the dragon swung its head, blazing red eyes fixing on Harry. Its wings twitched. And it was moving again, gliding towards him, jaws opening a second time …

Harry tumbled backwards, dragged by Ava. He lost touch with the hull completely and saw why – Ava had cut the cord. They were floating free,

spinning and tumbling away from the
Nersepha.

"Help!" he cried in panic.

"Hold on," Ava called, grabbing him.
He felt a tug, and realised she'd fired
up the thrusters on her boots. They
shot away, clinging to one another. Up
ahead, he spotted the Intercept IV, still
hovering. He felt a rush of relief. Admiral
Achebe hadn't left her daughter in
danger after all.

"Incoming tractor beam." The
Admiral's voice crackled over their
communicators. Then a ray of blue light
shot from the spacecraft, and Harry felt
himself being hauled in along with Ava.

A moment later, the tractor hatch

closed behind them. Ava lay there, panting. But Harry leapt to his feet and pushed his way past the rescued cadets to the viewing window.

Pressing his face up against it, he watched in astonishment.

The dragon had coiled itself around the *Nersepha*, its wings folded tightly, like a spider wrapping a fly up in silk. Harry shuddered. The dragon's body seemed to be pulsing with flashes of green. It was almost as though it was feeding – absorbing something from the ship.

The pulsing stopped. For a moment, all was still …

Then the dragon flexed its coils,

crumpling up the transport ship as easily as tin foil. Gasps of horror rose up from the cadets.

The dragon shimmered away, melting into space as though it had been a mirage all along.

Harry blinked, trying to take it all in.

What just happened?

CHAPTER 7

SWARM BOTS

"Ready the Moat guns!" barked
Admiral Achebe. "All hands to the
emergency gun turrets!"

The Admiral was striding so fast
through the corridors of Vantia1 that
Harry had to jog to keep up with her.
Everywhere, the emergency lights

glowed a dim blood-red. *High Alert.*

At any other time, he would have felt a flush of pride to be walking alongside Governor Knox, Admiral Achebe and Zo Harkman. Receiving salutes, as though he were one of them. But all he could think about was the horror of that dragon, coiling around the transport ship before crushing it to space scrap.

"We must evacuate," said Bremmer, keeping pace with the Governor. He looked deathly pale, even in the red light. "Send all personnel to the nearest station."

Governor Knox waved him away impatiently. "We can't launch innocent people with that *thing* waiting out there."

"And we can't leave Vantia1 defenceless," said Achebe.

On the gun deck, Harry saw cargo workers shifting trolleys of blaster cells to the Moat cannons. Engineers were running checks and increasing the calibre of the guns.

Gunners themselves were fine-tuning their targeting headsets. Everyone looked tense. On edge. *There hasn't been an attack on the station since ...* Harry frowned. *Well. Ever.*

Governor Knox led them to a Mole pod and requested the Bridge, as the main Observation Deck was called. It was situated at the top of the station. Even the pod was bathed in red light as they rose, in silence.

The doors slid open.

"Whoa!" said Harry.

The others strode out, but it took him a moment to take it all in. The Bridge was thirty metres across, and covered in a transparent dome which gave a 360-degree view on all sides. There were banks of consoles manned by numerous personnel, all working hard and muttering into their headsets. In the centre was a platform dominated by a swivel chair for whoever was in charge. Governor Knox seated herself in it now. Zo went to another seat at her side, and Admiral Achebe remained standing.

Harry edged in, eyes fixed on the millions of stars. There was no sign of any danger.

For now.

"Do you have any idea what it is?" he asked quietly.

Zo shook his head. The frown had not left his face since Harry had returned from the *Nersepha*. "That's what scares me. I've never seen anything like it before. It's like it was made by a different civilisation."

"And that is why we must try to understand it," said Governor Knox. "*Communicate* with it."

Harry turned, embarrassed that she had been listening in.

"Communicate ..." the Admiral muttered, shaking her head. "Perhaps a cannon blast would get the message across?"

Something flickered at the edge of Harry's vision. Something far out through the viewing dome, in the darkness. "What was that?" The hairs prickled at the back of his neck.

"Electromagnetic glitch," said one of the Observation Techs.

"Are you sure?" Harry couldn't help himself. "If we run an energy scan ..."

The Ob Tech frowned. "I really don't think that's necessary."

"Do it," growled Zo.

"Sir." The Ob Tech tapped at his screen.

The viewing screen shimmered, and a faint pink overlay appeared across it.

A soft sigh ran across the deck. The sound of everyone gasping at once.

A slithering shape was making its way towards the station, getting bigger all the time.

Governor Knox broke the silence.

"Why couldn't we see it before?"

But something was happening to the shape now. It was sparkling, glinting with bits of metal.

The Ob Tech removed the overlay. And now they could all see it – the dragon appearing out of nothingness, every part of it blinking into being, like iron filings locking into shape. Every so often, as its body twitched, it seemed to phase out of existence before reappearing again.

"A swarm!" cried Harry. Everyone turned to look at him. "That's how it can move without being seen. It's made up of thousands of tiny swarm bots. When they're separate, they're too small to be seen. But when they come together ..."

"They create a robo-dragon," finished Zo. He nodded slowly. "The boy's right."

Harry couldn't help feeling a flicker of pride. There was no time for that, though.

"It's almost inside the Moat," said

Admiral Achebe. She'd barely finished speaking when bolts of green energy arced up from the automatic Moat gunnery, slicing through space.

Harry held his breath as the bolts struck the dragon. But instead of being blown apart, the dragon's body flexed and shimmered, absorbing the energy without the slightest bit of damage.

"What on all Avantia … ?" breathed the Admiral.

The robo-dragon's wings unfurled like flags. Then down it swooped, soaring like an eagle. It opened its jaws, spewing a torrent of blue plasma that bathed the gun turrets in a crackling light. The entire Observation Deck glowed blue for an instant.

Harry blinked. When he looked again, the Moat's gun turrets were a smouldering, half-melted mess. He felt sick, and dizzy with awe.

Zo stared, open-mouthed in horror. No amount of engineering skill was going to fix the gun turrets *this* time.

"Launch defence ships," said the Governor. "Quickly!"

Admiral Achebe reeled out orders into her communicator. Seconds later, Harry saw the first of the silver craft zipping from the Flight Deck like wasps defending their nests. Energy bolts darted from their onboard cannons. The dragon writhed to dodge the attacks.

"Those cannons won't do a thing," said Zo quietly.

Sure enough, the dragon's body absorbed the energy bolts that *did* hit, just as it had with the Moat guns. It lashed its tail, twisting round and diving at the attacking craft, which scattered like leaves on the breeze as the dragon pursued. It caught one with its tail, ripping it apart in a flare of exploding fuel.

Admiral Achebe walked up close to the viewing dome, her mouth hanging open, and laid a hand against the glass. "How are we supposed to beat this thing?"

Harry crossed to an empty console.

Tapping at the controls, he brought up the scans of the dragon. Rotated. Zoomed.

An idea was forming in his mind.

"They're communicating," he muttered.

"What's that, Harry?"

He looked up into Zo's concerned eyes. "The swarm," said Harry. "They have to be communicating with each other. Otherwise, the dragon would come apart."

Zo's eyes shone. "So if we can disrupt their communication ..."

"Then we can destroy it," Harry finished, his heart pounding. *It's not going to be easy ... but it might work.*

"A.D.U.R.O.," said Zo. "Scan for comm frequencies in the vicinity of the attack."

"Scanning," said A.D.U.R.O., calmly – like this was not a life-or-death situation at all.

Harry looked up at the viewing dome again. The dragon had the Vantian spacecraft on the run. It sliced with a wing, smashing three of them at once and sending them whirling away.

The dragon swerved right past the station. It was so close that Harry could see its glowing red eyes. Plasma erupted from its jaws again, scorching a lower deck with a long stream of blue fire.

One of the Ob Techs looked up with

fear in his eyes. "We've got breaches on Decks 3 and 4. Authorising emergency evacuation protocols."

Banking again, the dragon flexed its wings and landed on one of the towers, ripping at the station's shell with its claws. The whole station seemed to shudder with the rending of metal, as damage reports flooded the Ob Techs' screens.

"Breach on Tower 3, Governor ..."

"Bulkheads 17 and 18 are compromised."

"It's heading for the Flight Deck!"

Peering through the viewing dome, Harry caught his breath. Whole chunks of metal had been ripped away and warped out of shape. Vantians were drifting free from the wreckage like tiny dust motes in their space-skins, flailing hopelessly.

Harry couldn't believe his eyes.

Vantia1. A safe haven for all the exiled people of Avantia.

It's being torn to pieces!

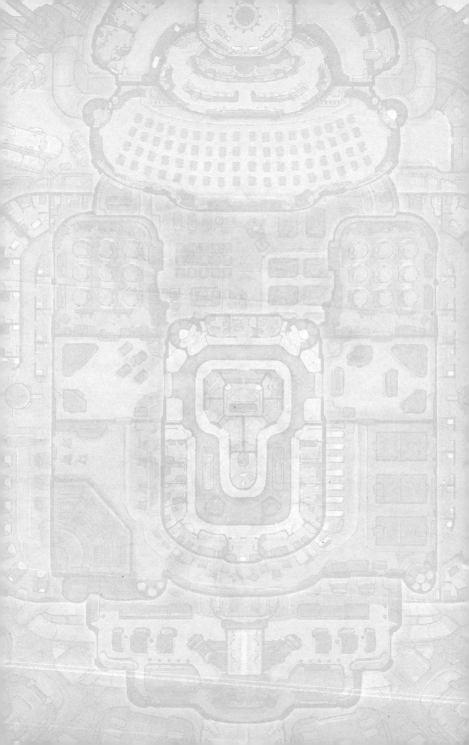

CHAPTER 8

SLINGSHOT

The dragon crawled across the outer shell of Vantia1, clinging on with its claws. Its tail lashed at the viewing windows. It opened its mouth and released another storm of blue plasma, frying a squadron of ships as they left the Flight Deck.

"Cadets, move out," ordered Admiral Achebe. "Take over any vessel you can find. Bring in anyone adrift."

Harry turned to look at the senior officers of Vantia1. Governor Knox, Admiral Achebe and Zo Harkman weren't doing a thing – just staring in utter dismay at what was happening.

Watching.

But I can't watch any more.

"Admiral! I need my Space Stallion." Normally he wouldn't dream of speaking to Admiral Achebe like that. But there was nothing normal about any of this.

The Admiral glared at him. "Stand down, Harry. There are enough Vantians in danger without—"

Harry didn't stick around to hear more. He was already darting out of the room. No one followed him into the corridor – not even Zo. *They've got bigger things to worry about.*

He entered a Mole pod and asked for the Flight Deck. At the same time, pulling up his sleeve, he thumbed a codepad on his robotic forearm to summon the Space Stallion to him. A slight shudder ran through the metal, as the emergency homing signal was dispatched.

"Come here, boy," he muttered.

Doubt flickered through his mind. *How am I going to get through a docking bay with no pass?*

KERRRUNCH!

The sound of screeching metal came from all around and for a moment nothing made sense. The pod shook from side to side, throwing him about, until suddenly there was no gravity at all and he was floating. Another thump tore it open on one side and cold washed over him. Outside there was … space. Harry pressed his belt button to inflate his space-skin.

He realised what had happened as the dragon soared past. It had ripped a hole in the side of the station and exposed the Mole channel! Just as he was wondering what to do, Harry saw a red and chrome streak coming to a halt beside him.

"Trouble round these parts?" said the Space Stallion.

"You could say that." Harry swung his leg  over the saddle and twisted the throttle, feeling the familiar thrum of the bike beneath him.

He swung the handlebars round so he could look back on Vantia1.

The sight took his breath away. Huge chunks of the station had been torn apart. Here and there, he could see straight into the decks, like it was a doll's house. Vantians were still drifting free. But now there were vessels among them, piloted by cadets, using tractor beams to haul the marooned people on board.

It was his home. *And that Space Dragon is destroying it!*

"Communication frequency identified."

It was A.D.U.R.O.'s voice, crackling from his communicator.

"The swarm channel," gasped Harry. "Can you disrupt it?"

"Negative, Harry. Remote disruption is impossible."

"But manual? That would work?"

"Correct," said A.D.U.R.O. "The source of the frequency transmitter is within the attacker."

Perfect.

"Harry!" This time it was Zo's voice, and he did not sound happy. "Get back here right now!"

Forcing away his guilt, Harry killed the channel.

His stomach lurched as he saw the Space Dragon soar out from behind the far side of Vantla1. It was even bigger than he'd imagined, its body glittering in the reflection of the blue plasma fires it had set.

The dragon circled above the station, watching its destruction. Then it dived down and ripped another chunk of outer shell away with its teeth.

Something was exposed now, glowing red from deep within Vantia1. It was an orb, almost as big as the dragon itself, held in place with a web of metal struts and cables.

The power core!

Harry's blood ran cold. The dragon wasn't just attacking mindlessly. And as it unleashed more blue flame, bursting across the surface of the power core, Harry understood its plan.

If the station's power core overheats, it will set off a chain reaction ... The whole station will explode ... Everyone on board will die!

There would be no second chances. *We have to stop it. Right now.*

He used the Stallion's console to change his communicator to the cadet channel. "Ava?" he said. "Come in, Ava."

She had to be there, on board one of the cadet vessels. Sure enough, her voice came through a moment later. "Harry? I'm kind of busy right now!"

"I know! But I've got a plan." He licked his lips. "I can destroy the dragon. But I need to get close. *Really* close. Can you distract it?"

Ava snorted. "You're crazy."

"Maybe," said Harry. "But 'crazy' worked last time, didn't it?"

Silence on the communicator. Harry

held his breath. "Fine," said Ava, at last. "Let's trash this heap of space junk."

Harry's heart leapt as one of the smaller vessels broke away from the fleet. It barrelled straight at the dragon, pelting it with rapid-fire green energy bolts.

The dragon twisted, flicking its wings to deflect the attack.

Harry opened up the throttle and swooped down towards the station. He swerved, veering on to the dragon's blind side.

Taking his metal hand off the bars, he reached under his saddle. The Stallion didn't have any on-board weaponry – just a spare fuel cell. *It'll have to do.*

Harry hefted it, a canister not much bigger than a football.

With any luck, that thing will be so busy defending itself from Ava that—

The dragon's body flickered. Then it exploded into a fine grey mist and re-formed, faster than he could have imagined. Looking right at Harry.

Its red eyes glowed.

Harry froze. The dragon was huge. So big, it blotted out everything else – the stars, the space station … even the Void.

Then it came for him, rushing through space, its metallic jaws yawning wide …

No second chances.

It was just like playing a game of slingshot on the Cargo Deck, surrounded by his friends. He hadn't missed once.

He wouldn't miss this time.

Taking aim, Harry threw the canister as hard as he could, straight at the dragon's mouth.

There was no time to check if it was a bullseye. He kicked away, flinging himself free. He glanced back, and saw the Stallion collide with the dragon and explode into fragments. As the sparks and smoke cleared, the creature turned to face him.

His blood ran cold. *It didn't work. This is it.*

WHUMPH! The dragon's belly flared white. It floundered, coiling as though it was in pain. Patches of its flesh

shimmered, breaking apart and re-forming. *It's happening!* Harry realised, feeling his heart lift in triumph. *The swarm can't communicate!*

Spikes of red light speared from inside the dragon, becoming brighter until Harry had to squint. Then, in a silent explosion, the dragon's whole body disintegrated. A wave of energy hit Harry, hurling him away so fast he felt like he was being pulled apart. His space-skin was shredding like wet cardboard as he was sent hurtling through the darkness.

When he tried to breathe, the oxygen wasn't flowing any more. Even through his panic, he understood. The skin had failed. The air was gone.

His chest tightened. His lungs were bursting.

And then everything …

… went …

… black.

CHAPTER 9

JUST A LITTLE REVENGE

"Harry?"

He was swimming through darkness, rising towards a bright light.

"Harry!"

A distant hum of consoles. Regular bleeps, matching his heartbeat.

"He's waking up!"

Where am I? He opened one eyelid. Flinched at the brightness. Then slowly opened the other.

The room blurred into focus around him. It was sterile white, with fluorescent lights overhead. Robot medics whirred here and there.

The infirmary.

He lay in bed, wires hooked up to sensors on his chest, head and arms. Everything ached. His mouth felt dry.

But he was alive.

"Are you OK?"

It was Ava who spoke. She stood by the bed, dressed in her cadet uniform. It was blackened and singed across one sleeve, as though she hadn't changed since the fight against the robo-dragon.

Harry felt a flood of relief at seeing her safe. "I was … worried …" he croaked.

Another, taller figure appeared at Ava's shoulder. It was Admiral Achebe – and to Harry's astonishment, she was smiling. "*You* were worried?" she said. "Ava wasn't the one blown up and drifting through space."

Harry didn't know what to say to that.

"You did it, Harry," said the Admiral, softly. "You destroyed the dragon. Everyone's safe, barring a few bruises and fractures among the Intercept pilots. Zero fatalities. All thanks to you."

Harry blinked. "Am I … dreaming?"

"No." Ava chuckled. "And there's more." She looked expectantly at her mother.

Admiral Achebe cleared her throat. "Indeed. The council has been impressed with you, Harry. More than impressed. You're thirteen in five days, I hear."

"Yes," said Harry.

"Well, in that case, I'd like to offer you a permanent position … on the cadet force."

Harry raised himself slowly up on to one elbow. His head swam, and he fought off a rush of nausea. "Really?"

"Really."

He couldn't believe it. Fighting

alongside the
defenders
of Vantia1 –
cadets like
Ava … and
Markus …
He frowned,
wondering how
Markus would take the news. *Not well*, he
guessed. But that didn't matter.

"Where's Zo?" he asked. "I'll have to
ask him first." *He can't say "no", not after
all this …*

"He's in Cargo Bay 9," said Admiral
Achebe. Her expression darkened. "He's
carrying out some … investigations."

"Can I see him?" asked Harry. "Please?"

The Admiral checked the diagnostic screen, then nodded. "It looks like you're well on your way to a full recovery."

"Tough as old rocket boots," said Ava. And she flashed him a grin.

✪

When the Mole dropped them on the Cargo Deck, there were a lot more security personnel than normal. Clearly something was up. Admiral Achebe escorted them towards Bay 9. A stack of crates formed a wall, blocking it from view, but Harry's eyes spotted his Space Stallion, propped up on supports in the corner. He rushed over, heart sinking. The chassis was bent and crumpled. He tried to power up, but circuits fizzed and

LEDs blinked randomly.

"Howdy, part-part-partner," said the Stallion, its voice crackling in and out like static. "Guess I'm bust-bust-busted real g-g-good."

Harry patted the Stallion's saddle. "Nothing I can't fix," he promised. "We'll have you back on the trail in no time."

"Harry ..."

He turned to see Ava. She was gesturing from ahead, past the wall of crates, and he walked over to join her.

The bay beyond was huge, with a vast metal floor and mobile consoles wheeled into place all around, linked up with cables. Zo Harkman was at one of them, with a couple of engineers, talking earnestly to Governor Knox and Secretary Bremmer. A.D.U.R.O. hovered at their side.

Taking up most of the bay floor were the remains of the robo-dragon, laid out like the bones of some ancient dinosaur.

Harry felt a strange mixture of wonder and fear to see the creature so close up.

It was utterly still, its body gleaming in the harsh light of the cargo bay. There was a gaping hole where its belly should have been, and its red eyes had blinked out at last.

When Zo saw them, he strode over at once and wrapped Harry up in a tight, powerful hug.

Harry hugged him back. He had never

been so relieved to see Zo before.

"Have you found out what it is?" he asked, when they finally stepped apart.

Zo's expression was grim. "We can't even work out what it's made of. The metal alloy is ... Well, it's unusual, to say the least."

"One thing is clear," said Governor Knox sternly. "Its objective was to destroy our station. And since it has no brain of its own, that means it was being controlled by someone else."

"Which means we have an enemy," said Admiral Achebe. "Unknown ... and powerful. If we could just find out who it is ..." She turned her gaze to the vast bulk of the dragon.

"Maybe we can," said Harry.

Everyone turned to look at him.

"I mean ..." He blushed, feeling suddenly awkward. "If we give the dragon a jolt – bring it back to life, just for a few moments ..."

Zo stroked his chin thoughtfully. "An electromagnetic pulse should do it. Controlled, of course."

"Are you mad?" Ava frowned fiercely. "That ... *thing* nearly killed us all!"

"We can use a low current," said Harry. "It won't be fully operational."

"Proceed," said Governor Knox quietly. "We have to find out more. One way or another."

Zo's engineers got to work, wiring up

the dragon's body.

"Stand by," said Zo, his fingers dancing across a control pad. Harry noticed Bremmer edging quietly away from the dragon. "3 ... 2 ... 1 ..."

Fffzzzapp! The dragon lurched suddenly, making everyone stumble backwards in shock.

Then, to Harry's astonishment, the body began to move. It melted into a sludge, coming together into a heap of silver. Then it grew taller still, until from its centre a column rose, like a snake rearing up.

"What's happening?" said Governor Knox, her voice hoarse.

No one replied.

The metal was flowing into the shape of a figure. A man. At first the features were indistinct, but slowly a face formed, with a short beard and a bald head. He was entirely silver, just like the dragon had been. But his glittering metal eyes were red, and sent a shiver down Harry's spine. There was something about them. Something ... *evil*.

"Who …" muttered Admiral Achebe, "… is that?"

"Vellis?"

Harry looked up to see that it was Zo who spoke. He was gaping at the metal man, jaw hanging open in astonishment. "Vellis – is it you?"

"Zo Harkman," the voice boomed and echoed through the cavernous cargo bay, unnaturally loud. "Congratulations on your victory." He smiled. "I'm only sorry that it won't last."

"I don't understand." Zo looked as though he had seen a ghost. "You died. You were there, when the Void swallowed Avantia."

The man called Vellis laughed. "Of

course I was there. Do you think I would have missed it? I've always thought the Void was my finest work."

Harry's heart began to hammer in his chest. "What does he mean?" he asked. But everyone was too busy staring at Vellis to reply.

"What do you want with us?" Governor Knox demanded.

Vellis showed his palms. "Oh, nothing much. Just a little *revenge*. Vengeance on all Vantians – the fools who never understood my genius. You will soon, of course. But by then, I'm afraid it will be too late." He leaned forward, his eyes blazing, hands curling into fists. "I'm going to destroy you all. Every … single … last …"

Fffffzzzap!

The man collapsed into a thousand metal shards, suddenly lifeless, until he was just a heap of fragments once more.

Turning, Harry saw that Zo had killed the power. He was pale and panting, his eyes wide.

There was a long, shocked silence.

"Chief Engineer Harkman?" said Governor Knox, at last. "Can you please explain?"

Zo nodded slowly. "That was Vellis," he said, in a low voice. "He was – is – a scientist. A brilliant one. But dangerous. He worked with … er …" Zo's gaze flickered to Harry. "Well. With Harry's parents."

Harry held his breath. He felt as though he was on the edge of something – something huge.

"He was supposed to be helping with their research into wormholes," Zo carried on. "But they fired him. You see, he was carrying out experiments of his own, in secret. Unsanctioned, unstable experiments. Whatever he did … it sent him mad." Zo sighed. "And somehow, it seems … he has survived the Void."

Harry stared at Zo. *All this time, he knew all of this … but he never said a word.*

He didn't know what to think.

Once again, it was Governor Knox who broke the silence. "Very good, Harkman," she said calmly. "Well, then. I think that's enough excitement for now. Let us hope that we never encounter this Vellis again."

Zo shot Harry a look of embarrassment – maybe even of apology. But Harry couldn't meet his eye for long.

Questions were racing through his mind. Could there be other survivors out there, in the Void? What *was* the Void? And had Vellis somehow created it?

If so, he was responsible for everything. For the loss of Avantia. All those lives. *My parents.*

He'd known that all along, deep in his bones, that it had never been their fault. It was almost too much to take in.

Harry gritted his teeth. He was exhausted, bruised and battered from the fight with the robo-dragon. But one thing was for sure.

If Vellis comes for us again … If he tries to destroy our home for a second time…

I'll be ready for him.

⭐

THE END

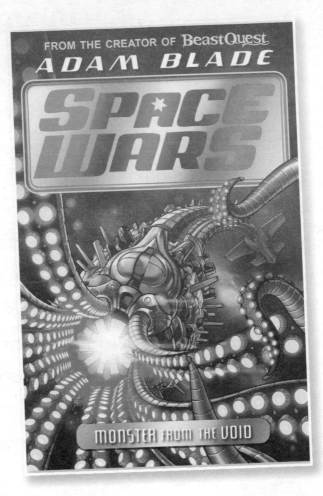

If you enjoyed this book, read on for
a sneak peek at Harry and Ava's next
amazing adventure ...

MONSTER FROM THE VOID

"Catch!" yelled Ava. She flung the ball, and it spun through the air in a flash.

"Got it," muttered Harry.

He had wired his prosthetic arm up to his rocket boots, and a twitch of his thumb sent power to the thrusters. A bit too much power. *WHOOOSH!* His heart lurched as he shot straight past the ball towards the wall of the game chamber.

He was too slow to manoeuvre and threw up his arms just in time to cushion the impact. *THUMP!*

Laughter echoed round the chamber as he righted himself. He saw a tall, blond-haired boy in the other team's colours intercept Ava's pass. *Markus Knox.* Harry gritted his teeth as his smug opponent flipped in the air, then hurled the ball towards the goal. The keeper flailed but failed to stop it.

"GOOOOAL!" The cry rang around the chamber. The glow-buoys flashed green and Markus did a victory somersault. A holographic scoreboard spun slowly above the court. *8-0.*

Harry groaned. Zero-G handball took some getting used to – especially with a new pair of rocket boots.

"Hey, Robo-arm, nice catch!" crowed Markus. He looped the loop, and Harry noticed that he was wearing Fireflash Rocket Hoppers – the best boots that credits could buy. *Boots I'd never be able to afford …*

"Pro tip," called Markus. "In the cadets, we try *not* to fly straight into walls." He grinned at his team-mates, but none of them seemed to find him all that funny.

Harry clenched his fists. His cheeks burned. But before he could answer back, Ava's hand closed over his arm. "Hey! You're new to the cadets, remember? This is the first time you've even played. You're doing great." Harry felt a little calmer, looking into her kind brown eyes. But he could still hear Markus behind her.

READ
MONSTER FROM THE VOID
TO FIND OUT WHAT HAPPENS...